KIDS CAN'T STOP READING THE CHOOSE YOUR OWN ADVENTURE® STORIES!

"Choose Your Own Adventure is the best thing that has come along since books themselves."

—Alysha Beyer, age 11

"I didn't read much before, but now I read my Choose Your Own Adventure books almost every night."

—Chris Brogan, age 13

"I love the control I have over what happens next."

—Kosta Efstathiou, age 17

"Choose Your Own Adventure books are so much fun to read and collect—I want them all!"

—Brendan Davin, age 11

And teachers like this series, too:

"We have read and reread, worn thin, loved, loaned, bought for others, and donated to school libraries our Choose Your Own Adventure books."

CHOOSE YOUR OWN ADVENTURE®— AND MAKE READING MORE FUN!

Bantam Books in the Choose Your Own Adventure® series
Ask your bookseller for the books you have missed

#1 THE CAVE OF TIME
#2 JOURNEY UNDER THE SEA
#3 DANGER IN THE DESERT
#4 SPACE AND BEYOND
#5 THE CURSE OF THE HAUNTED MANSION
#6 SPY TRAP
#7 MESSAGE FROM SPACE
#8 DEADWOOD CITY
#9 WHO KILLED HARLOWE THROMBEY?
#10 THE LOST JEWELS
#22 SPACE PATROL
#31 VAMPIRE EXPRESS
#52 GHOST HUNTER
#53 THE CASE OF THE SILK KING
#66 SECRET OF THE NINJA
#71 SPACE VAMPIRE
#75 PLANET OF THE DRAGONS
#76 THE MONA LISA IS MISSING!
#77 THE FIRST OLYMPICS
#78 RETURN TO ATLANTIS
#79 MYSTERY OF THE SACRED STONES
#80 THE PERFECT PLANET
#81 TERROR IN AUSTRALIA
#82 HURRICANE!
#83 TRACK OF THE BEAR
#84 YOU ARE A MONSTER
#85 INCA GOLD
#86 KNIGHTS OF THE ROUND TABLE
#87 EXILED TO EARTH
#88 MASTER OF KUNG FU
#89 SOUTH POLE SABOTAGE
#90 MUTINY IN SPACE
#91 YOU ARE A SUPERSTAR
#92 RETURN OF THE NINJA
#93 CAPTIVE!
#94 BLOOD ON THE HANDLE
#95 YOU ARE A GENIUS
#96 STOCK CAR CHAMPION
#97 THROUGH THE BLACK HOLE
#98 YOU ARE A MILLIONAIRE
#99 REVENGE OF THE RUSSIAN GHOST
#100 THE WORST DAY OF YOUR LIFE
#101 ALIEN, GO HOME!
#102 MASTER OF TAE KWON DO
#103 GRAVE ROBBERS
#104 THE COBRA CONNECTION
#105 THE TREASURE OF THE *ONYX DRAGON*
#106 HIJACKED!
#107 FIGHT FOR FREEDOM
#108 MASTER OF KARATE

#1 JOURNEY TO THE YEAR 3000 (A Choose Your Own Adventure Super Adventure)
#2 DANGER ZONES (A Choose Your Own Adventure Super Adventure)

CHOOSE YOUR OWN ADVENTURE® • 108

MASTER OF KARATE

BY RICHARD BRIGHTFIELD

ILLUSTRATED BY FRANK BOLLE

An Edward Packard Book

A BANTAM SKYLARK BOOK®
NEW YORK • TORONTO • LONDON • SYDNEY • AUCKLAND

This is a work of fiction. All of the characters and events in this book are imaginary. Any resemblance to real people or companies is entirely coincidental.

RL 4, age 10 and up

MASTER OF KARATE
A Bantam Book / December 1990

CHOOSE YOUR OWN ADVENTURE® is a registered trademark of Bantam Books, a division of Bantam Doubleday Dell Publishing Group, Inc. Registered in U.S. Patent and Trademark Office and elsewhere.

Original conception of Edward Packard

Cover art by David Mattingly
Interior illustrations by Frank Bolle

ISBN 0-553-28202-6

Published simultaneously in the United States and Canada

Bantam Books are published by Bantam Books, a division of Bantam Doubleday Dell Publishing Group, Inc. Its trademark, consisting of the words "Bantam Books" and the portrayal of a rooster, is Registered in U.S. Patent and Trademark Office and in other countries. Marca Registrada. Bantam Books, 666 Fifth Avenue, New York, New York 10103.

PRINTED IN THE UNITED STATES OF AMERICA

OPM 0 9 8 7 6 5 4 3 2 1

For Susan Korman,
Charles Kochman,
Emi Ohki, and
Akiko Seto

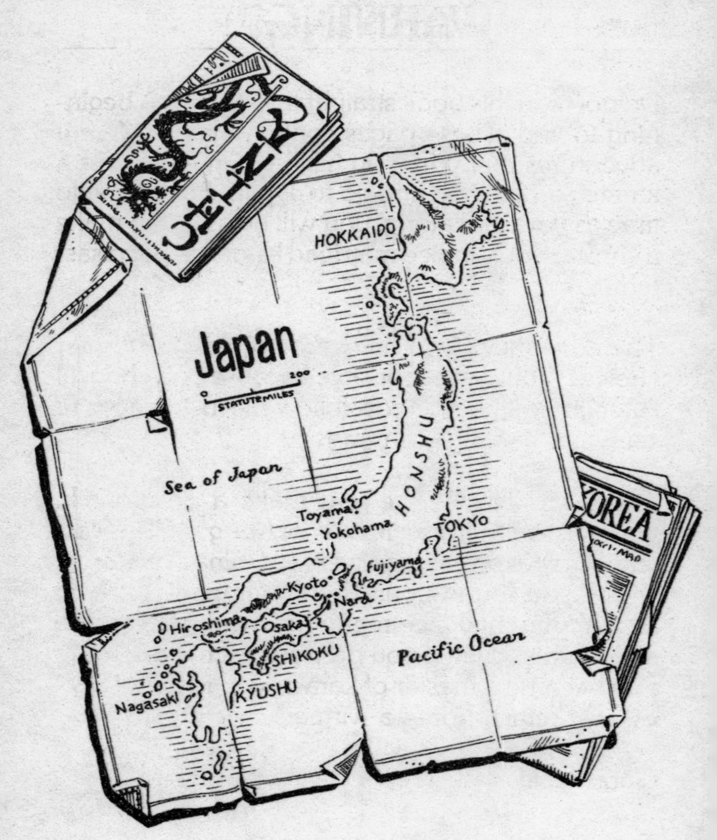

Japan
200
0
STATUTE MILES
HOKKAIDO
HONSHU
Sea of Japan
Toyama
Yokohama
TOKYO
Fujiyama
Kyoto
Nara
Hiroshima
Osaka
SHIKOKU
KYUSHU
Nagasaki
Pacific Ocean
KOREA

WARNING!!!

Do not read this book straight through from beginning to end. These pages contain many different adventures that you may have when you enter a karate competition and go to Japan. From time to time as you read along, you will be asked to make a choice. Your choice may lead to success or disaster!

The adventures you have are the results of your choices. You are responsible because you choose! After you make a choice, follow the instructions to see what happens to you next.

Think carefully before you make a decision. In your past adventures, *Master of Kung Fu* and *Master of Tae Kwon Do,* you went to China and Korea, where you found yourself in great peril. Now, in Japan, you may face many new and unexpected adventures. Even if you do win the championship and become a master of karate, you may not necessarily return home a winner!

Good luck!

BOYS
LOCKER
ROOM
COACH
KARATE
3:00
GYM

You are nodding off in Ms. McGrath's English class, the last class of the day, when the school bell finally rings. You collect your books and head for the door, then rush down the wide corridor toward the gym.

Seconds later, you're at your hall locker, stowing away your books and pulling out your *gi*, a white, loose-fitting karate uniform. In the locker room, you change as fast as you can and run into the gym where the other members of the karate club—of which you are the president—are already lined up in a row. Billy Baxter, your best friend, is there after having dropped out of the club for a year to concentrate on computers. You take your place next to him at the head of the line and nod hello to Veronica Martin, a new but very promising member.

Mr. Clark, your gym teacher and faculty adviser for the karate club, enters. Everyone stops talking as he kneels down on the floor in front of you. One by one you and your classmates do the same, preparing for the brief session of meditation that always begins your after-school practice. At the signal you close your eyes and "try to wipe the mirror of your mind free of dust," as Mr. Clark likes to say, quoting one of the ancient Chinese masters.

After meditation, you all stand and bow before Mr. Clark, who bows back in return. He studied karate in Japan when he was in the army, and he likes to include all the formalities that he learned over there.

Turn to page 2.

2

"Before we start today's practice," Mr. Clark says, "I have an announcement to make. UJEC, a Japanese electronics company, is sponsoring a nationwide karate tournament. We have been asked to compete. The qualifying meet will be held at a school in Middletown two weeks from now, and the finals will take place in Japan, with all expenses paid for by UJEC. I suggest that we work extra hard to prepare."

After practice, you, Billy, and Veronica walk home. "Winning that tournament should be a snap," Billy says to you. "After all, we both studied kung fu with the best in China, and you learned a lot about tae kwon do last summer in Korea while searching for your friend Ling. Our martial arts training is pretty strong."

"That doesn't mean that someone else might not have as much training or as much skill," you say.

"You two are the best in our class," Veronica says. "I'm just a beginner, but if they count the whole team in the scoring, then—"

"Don't worry," Billy interrupts. "You're good. If you continue to practice, you can only get better."

"We have two weeks," you say. "Instead of our usual three times a week, let's promise to practice together every day. Even if it's only for an hour."

"I'm with you," Billy says.

"Count me in," says Veronica, waving goodbye and turning up the driveway to her house.

Go on to the next page.

Two weeks later, you and the rest of your karate team meet at Middletown High. The bleachers set up on the sides of the gym are packed with spectators, and in the center, a large square ring is marked off on the floor with a broad white border. Teams from a dozen schools in the state are gathered, broken off into groups, all around the ring.

Mr. Tanaka, a gentleman from UJEC, comes to the judges' table and announces in broken English the basic rules and the start of the tournament. Contestants are paired off into individual and team matches according to an elimination chart drawn up earlier from a random selection of names. Each bout will last three minutes or until a major punch or kick is delivered just short of actual contact.

The lineup begins with Veronica, to be followed by Billy in the second match. Veronica wins, but Billy loses, a little too easily for his earlier bravado. "I guess I need more practice than I thought," he says, walking over dejectedly to where you and the team are grouped.

After that, of the other six members on your team, five win and one loses. It's your turn next. The team now has enough points to carry the tournament if you win the match!

Go on to the next page.

You go to the center of the ring and assume a fighting stance. At the judge's signal your opponent, a tall blond boy with a crew cut, attacks almost at once. You quickly dodge his attack and grab his sleeve, throwing him off balance. Then you counterattack with a backhand strike to a point a quarter of an inch from the bridge of his nose. After a succession of quick punches and kicks that drive your opponent out of the ring, the referee calls for the end of the match and declares you the winner.

The crowd goes wild as Mr. Tanaka congratulates you and your team, shaking your hands. "Wow!" Veronica exclaims. "We did it."

A few weeks later you, Billy, and Veronica are driven to the airport by your mother. "Be careful," she says. "Remember what happened to you while you were away on your other trips."

"Don't worry," you say. "What kind of trouble could I get into this time?"

In the terminal, you meet Mr. Clark and the rest of the team, then you board your Japan Airlines flight to Tokyo. Billy bends your ear about computers for almost the whole flight over. "This trip will be fantastic," he says. "The Japanese produce some great computers, not to mention all the other electronic stuff they make." He seems to have forgotten all about karate and the reason you are going to Japan. Veronica, on the other hand, sleeps for most of the flight. In a way, you envy her.

Turn to page 34.

The salesclerk slams the door shut and locks it behind him. He begins hollering something in Japanese into a phone, but it must be dead, because he throws it to the floor with disgust.

"Must hide or run away," he says in English. "Bad samurai come, break up store." He points to a door that seems to lead to the basement, then points to a back door that leads outside.

Meanwhile the bad samurai are trying to smash through the showroom door. It's starting to splinter. You could run out the back door, but there may be more samurai waiting out there. On the other hand, you could escape to the basement only to find yourself trapped down there. Whatever you choose, you have to decide fast!

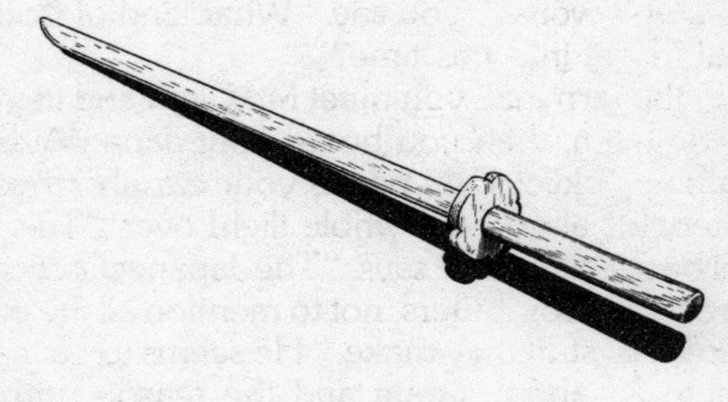

If the three of you hide in the basement, turn to page 54.

If you run out the back door, turn to page 71.

You and Aikiko grab a large recessed ring in the trapdoor and pull it up. You can hear the bell ringing at the gate outside.

"This was a bomb shelter during the war, when Tokyo and its suburbs were bombed. Fortunately, this was one of the few houses not destroyed," the baroness says, looking over her shoulder.

You and Aikiko climb down a ladder, into the dark chamber. "There is a flashlight on the wall," the baroness calls to you. A moment later the door closes over your head.

You feel along the wall. "Here it is," you say, clicking the light on and shining it around the underground room.

Turn to page 48.

"Each of those cars must think that we're in the other one," Aikiko whispers. "Kokuru's men are always getting their communications fouled up."

"Lucky for us," you say as a tremendous explosion rips from up above, and a ball of flame rises into the air.

"I think somebody hit a gas tank," she says.

"We have nothing to worry about now," you say.

"We can't be sure of that. Many of Kokuru's men might not be too bright, but don't underestimate Kokuru himself. Besides, he owns the countryside around here. We still have a long way to go before we're free.

The drop-off below the road gives way to a moderate slope, wooded in spots. To the side you find a deer path and follow it down to level ground. Soon you're walking down narrow footpaths between cultivated fields. The night is buzzing with the sound of frogs and crickets. Clusters of houses lie ahead.

Turn to page 38.

As the two of you walk to the ring and face off, the hall becomes silent. It is the first time you take a good look at your opponent, and you can't believe your eyes—it's the man whose helmet you knocked off in the back of the electronics store! He's the one responsible for your being kidnapped!

You must decide what to do quickly. You could go on with the match as if there is nothing wrong. Or you could demand that the man be arrested.

If you decide to continue with the match,
turn to page 95.

If you excuse yourself and call the police,
turn to page 17.

Sometime later, the fisherman comes down again and unties you. Your arms and legs are sore from being tied up so long, but you must go up on deck and start helping the fishermen pull in the nets. Later, you are able to stop long enough to eat a bowl of fish soup with rice.

Weeks go by. To your surprise, you begin to like your new life at sea. Gradually you learn the language and the ways of the fishermen. Every few days one of them gives you a cup of that strange liquid to drink. Since you're unable to remember anything about your past, you no longer miss it. You work with them for many years to come, never sure of anything beyond your daily routine.

The End

An hour or so later, you pull up to the front of a huge, glass-walled building. After getting the room keys at the front desk, you follow Mr. Clark through the glittering lobby where you join the rest of the group.

"How does everyone feel?" Mr. Clark asks listlessly. "I'm going to turn in and sleep off some of this jet lag. If anyone goes out, don't stray too far from the hotel. Remember, we have to be up early tomorrow for practice." He turns around, then disappears into the elevator, followed by most of your group.

"I don't know about the two of you, but I'm going out and having a look around," you say.

"I'm with you," Billy says. "Maybe we can find a computer store."

"What *are* we going to do with you!" Veronica exclaims. "We just got here. Come, let's explore. Which way first?"

"Let's just walk in one direction and see what there is," you say. "We can come back and try another direction tomorrow."

As the three of you pass though the revolving door to the outside, you notice that the sun has vanished and it's starting to rain. The sky is almost as dark as night, and people all around you are opening umbrellas and racing for cover. In addition to the rain, there seems to be a smoggy haze in the air that blurs the cascades of red, orange, and yellow neon signs that run along both sides of the street.

Turn to page 91.

Inside is a spacious apartment decorated in the traditional Japanese style, with *tatami* mats on the floor and *shoji* screens dividing the room, all leading out to a small, open garden.

"Off to side here," Mr. Yoshi says, pointing, "is modern bathroom with Japanese tub. You will find futon mattress rolled up in cabinet. Radio and television are built into cabinet next to *tokonoma* alcove. Meals will be sent to you here."

"All this and room service too," you say sarcastically, smiling. Mr. Yoshi, however, doesn't smile. Maybe the joke was over his head, you think. In any event, he turns around and leaves the room.

Turn to page 96.

As the van backs out into the main street, the samurai figures tie your hands and feet, then blindfold you. You hope that Billy and Veronica managed to get away.

From somewhere in the distance, you can hear sirens coming. At the same time, the men in the van are arguing back and forth in Japanese. You can't understand what they are saying, but your guess is that they are talking about you.

You can feel the van moving slowly through traffic. It's not the fastest getaway, you imagine, but the police themselves probably can't move through the heavy Tokyo traffic any faster. The sirens, in fact, seem to be falling farther and farther behind.

You certainly have a lot of questions in your mind. Why the strange costumes? you wonder. And why the attack on the electronics store in the first place? More importantly, what are they going to do with you now that they have you?

After a while, the van starts to go faster, and you guess that you're out of the city. Your kidnappers have been quiet for some time. You feel the road going uphill. Finally, the van comes to a stop.

Turn to page 36.

You tell the invisible speaker your name. "I came to Japan to compete in a karate tournament," you say.

There is a pause. "Quite a coincidence then," the voice says. "Have interesting proposal for you. Have our own karate training program. You are invited to join. You do well to consider, keep open mind, and go along with us."

"What do I have to do?" you ask.

"You will find out when it is time. Your decision, please."

What should you do? you wonder. If you accept the offer, even if you pretend to join, will you be able to back out later on, or escape? On the other hand, if you say no, who knows what will happen to you?

If you decide to accept the offer,
turn to page 88.

If you decide to decline the offer,
turn to page 79.

The referee and your opponent stand there as you excuse yourself and run out of the ring. Using the phone in the dressing room, you call the number Inspector Saito gave you and leave a message for him with the police. Apologetic, you dash back just in time, and the referee doesn't eliminate you from the match.

Your opponent, you realize, will not be so easy to defeat. You can tell from the look in his eyes and the smooth, effortless way he moves that he is good; very good in fact. It takes all your skill to dodge his first attack. You shift to the side and close in, looking for an opening for a snap kick. He takes a flat-handed swipe at you as you jump back, but not quite fast enough. Something catches for a second in the loose-fitting sleeve of your gi and makes a small tear. Was it a needle or a small blade? you wonder. Your opponent tries to strike again, but you jump back even farther.

Turn to page 93.

Aikiko bows back and says something to her in Japanese. At the same time, she hands her a small calling card. "Luckily I always carry a few of my cards with me," Aikiko says to you. "It's an important custom."

"Your friend speaks English, no Japanese?" the woman asks. "Well, I am Baroness Yamoto. I have learned some of your language. Where are you from?"

"I'm here from the United States," you say. "I'm registered in a karate tournament."

"How nice," the baroness says. "Please, come, sit by the *tokonoma.* Yumiko will bring us some tea."

The baroness directs you and Aikiko to the front of a vertical alcove filled with a hanging scroll inscribed with Japanese calligraphy. Underneath it is a vase holding several carefully arranged flowers. "I am proud of my flower arrangements," she says. "It's my main pastime these days, other than writing letters to friends."

"Perhaps I could first use your phone," Aikiko asks. "Then I'll be able to relax and enjoy your tea."

Go on to the next page.

"Certainly. My late husband had a small office over here," the baroness says. She pulls back a shoji screen, revealing a small room with a desk and several bookcases built into the wall. "The phone is on the desk."

Aikiko slips into the room and picks up the phone.

"I still keep his office the way he left it," the baroness says to you. "My husband was killed in the war many years ago."

"I'm sorry," you say.

"Thank you," the baroness says. "My husband was opposed to the war. He admired much about your country, but it was too dangerous to speak openly with others. I alone knew what was in his heart. But whatever his personal beliefs, he was a soldier and loyal to the emperor."

Turn to page 42.

"I'll go back in with you, but—"

"Do not speak," Aikiko whispers. "Follow me and watch your footing."

You move along behind her, clinging to the side of the building. She makes her way to the corner and disappears around it. When you get there, you gingerly feel ahead with your foot, making sure the ledge continues on that side of the building. As you make the turn around the corner, you see in the moonlight that the ledge leads to a broad stone platform in the distance ahead.

When you finally reach the platform, Aikiko is waiting for you impatiently. "Hurry," she whispers. "We mustn't be seen out here. There are guards on watch above us."

A shaft of pale yellow light cuts momentarily into the darkness as Aikiko opens a door in the wall and pulls you inside. "I hope no one saw us," she says.

You find yourself in a wide hallway at the end of which is a bank of elevators, the kind you find in a hotel or an office building. Aikiko runs over and presses one of the buttons.

Turn to page 50.

"We here at UJEC are out to dominate the world, economically and technologically," Mr. Kokuru continues. "My misguided predecessors thought they could do this militarily, but of course they were proven wrong. War is nothing if not completely destructive. We intend to expand peacefully but relentlessly."

"Where do I fit into all this?" you ask, getting to the point yourself.

"Ah, yes," he says, rubbing his hands together. "It's in people like you that we place our hope for the future—not just Japanese, there are too few of us, but selected people throughout the world. By using our computers, we will find those who fit our requirements."

Mr. Kokuru shakes your hand again and heads back toward his desk. "Yoshi will explain the rest," he says as he leaves.

You follow Mr. Yoshi back out the door. "UJEC factories and laboratories all over Japan," he says. "In fact, all over world. But here at headquarters, we develop most advanced products and train top agents. Do you know Sun Tzu's book, *The Art of War*? It was written twenty-five hundred years ago. In it he outlines planning and conduct of military operations. Is still best book on subject."

"I thought Mr. Kokuru's plans were for a peaceful expansion," you say.

"They are," Mr. Yoshi says, changing the subject.

Turn to page 75.

At the end of the video, the audience rises and starts chanting in a kind of frenzy. The girl taps you on the shoulder and motions for you to follow her once again. You hurry after her as she rushes through a smaller doorway at the side of the auditorium and out into a hallway.

"Who are you and what is this all about?" you ask.

"My name is Aikiko. We will speak further, but right now I'm in a hurry," she says, directing you into a small room about the same size as the cell you were put into earlier. Aikiko leaves, and once again you're alone, left to wonder where you are and what will happen to you. This time, however, you notice a small window overhead. Some large boxes are lined up along the wall on one side. You could easily pile them up on top of one another and reach the window. But is this some kind of test? you wonder.

If you decide to try to get out of the window, turn to page 64.

If you decide to wait for Aikiko to come back, turn to page 100.

"Hey, wait a minute," you say. "I came over here with my friends to be in a karate tournament and—"

"You will be contacted soon about their true intentions," Niko says.

"If what you say is true, how did they know I'd win the qualifying meet back home?"

"With your martial arts background," Niko laughs, "how could you lose? Listen, We know about UJEC's plan to take over the world, but nothing specific. Need more precise information if we are going to . . . uh, take advantage of it ourselves. The Golden Ear Yakuza needs a spy in their organization, and you have been chosen. There's a lot of money in it for you."

"And if I refuse?" you say.

"But this is offer you *can't* refuse," Niko says. "But of course, the decision is yours."

Or is it, you wonder.

If you agree to be a spy for the Yakuza, turn to page 62.

If you refuse, turn to page 106.

You and Aikiko work your way around the main room, over to the veranda. From there you look down the garden path to the front gate. It's open, and you can see the front of a large car framed within it.

You look over the edge of the veranda, but your shoes are gone. Nevertheless you and Aikiko move quietly down to the side of the gate. Through a crack you can see that two men are in the front of the car, dozing.

Aikiko whispers in your ear, "My guess is that they've left the doors unlocked so that they can get out quickly if they need to. I think we need to attack. When I count to three, you take the one on the driver's side and I'll take the other one."

The two of you move over to the sides of the car. Holding up her fingers, Aikiko counts, "One, two, three."

Quickly you and Aikiko yank the doors open. The man on your side is so surprised that he almost falls out of the car by himself. You help him, grabbing hold of his collar and knocking him to the ground.

You look over and see Aikiko knock out the other man with a punch. "Hurry! Get in!" she says.

Soon you and Aikiko are speeding down the road.

Turn to page 41.

You step off the elevator and into a large laboratory filled with computers and elaborate electronic equipment and machines. Technicians in white lab coats are busily working inside Plexiglas enclosures, no doubt designed to control temperature as well as contain the sound.

"Kokuru is developing a computer chip the size of a pinhead," Aikiko whispers. "It will be planted in every type of UJEC equipment—radios, television sets, computers, telephones, fax machines, even digital wristwatches. Through it Kokuru will broadcast subliminal commands. People all over the world will be subconsciously programmed to buy only UJEC products and later to follow Kokuru's orders."

"But how can—" you start.

"Later," Aikiko interrupts. "Here comes trouble."

It's trouble all right. You recognize at once the man approaching in the black gi with a UJEC logo emblazoned in crimson on the chest—it's the man whose helmet you knocked off at the back of the store in Tokyo! He begins shouting at Aikiko in Japanese. Then he calls over another man, also dressed in black. Calmly, Aikiko answers both their questions.

Turn to page 45.

"Tell me about it," you say.

"I represent the management of the UJEC," he says. "We want you to do some work for us. We'll give you training, accommodations, all expenses paid."

"But why me?" you ask as the limousine pulls away from the curb.

"You are good. Very good. We've had an eye on you for a very long time. We know about your previous trips to China and Korea. You are a very strong fighter."

"That's flattering, but what about the tournament?"

"You do not need karate tournament. It is more important that you work for us. We will arrange everything."

"But what about my friends? Can they be included in this?" you ask.

"Have offer for friends as well. But that will come later. Not wise to put cart before horse, as people in your country say."

"What exactly do you want me to do?"

"As I say, we give you special training. We take you now to our castle."

Turn to page 70.

You are now some distance into the suburbs, which seem to stretch on forever. You see housing complexes mixed with factories pouring smoke into the air and in the far distance, rising out of the smog, the perfect cone of Mt. Fuji. Soon the countryside turns more rural, and you begin to see farms. Up ahead, on a high hill, a large, gleaming white building with dark, slanting roofs seems to soar up into the sky.

"That is castle," Mr. Yoshi says. "It dates back to the Yamoto family, but it is now headquarters of the UJEC."

Soon you are going up a long, winding road to the front of the castle. It has a moat and a drawbridge just like the ones you've read about. But the similarity ends there. Instead of towers and battlements, there are high white walls that rise up into the overhanging roofs.

The car drives across the drawbridge and into the castle. It stops inside a large, high-ceilinged garage, and you and Mr. Yoshi get out. He then leads you to a bank of elevators at the far side.

"I will show you to your quarters," he says. "I'm sure you will find them satisfactory."

The elevator goes up several floors, then comes to a stop. Mr. Yoshi leads you down a long hallway to a door at the end.

Turn to page 13.

"There's no way I'm staying here," you say. "I'm going with you."

Aikiko nods as the door to the elevator opens and the two of you step out. Not far away, a mechanic is working on a large truck, its hood up and the motor running.

As Aikiko rushes toward him, the man sees her and straightens up, a wrench in his hand. He makes a swipe at her just as she leaves the ground and connects with a snap kick to his chest. The mechanic goes flying backward over a workbench and into the wall behind it. He's out cold.

Aikiko slams the hood of the truck shut and runs around to the driver's side. "Jump in, quick!" she shouts.

Turn to page 89.

"Excuse our impoliteness for whispering," the baroness says, "but Yumiko has a premonition that some men are approaching on a nearby road. There have been times in the past when she has been known to have psychic powers."

"If she's right, we'd better do something quick," you say.

"Come, follow me." The baroness leads you into the office and pulls back one of the tatami mats. Underneath, there is the outline of a trap-door.

"You must help me with this," she says. "It is very heavy."

Turn to page 6.

Hoping to be able to use the phone, you ring the bell at the front gate. After a short wait, a woman in a plain kimono, younger than the other one you saw, opens the gate slightly and peers outside.

"Tosuke Ga Irimasuka?" she asks.

Aikiko speaks with her in Japanese. The woman nods and closes the gate again. "She wanted to know what we wanted. I told her we had an automobile accident on the road and would like to use her phone," Aikiko says.

You can faintly hear a discussion in Japanese going on inside the house. "Can you tell what they are saying?" you ask.

"It's hard to make out," Aikiko says, "but—"

The gate suddenly opens again, this time all the way. The younger woman bows and says something in Japanese. You and Aikiko follow her through the garden.

On your left, a small waterfall cascades down the face of a miniature mountain. Along the edge of the pond, a stone lantern lights your way. You and Aikiko leave your shoes at the edge of the garden and step up onto the veranda. Its wooden surface is highly polished and leads up to an area of the house where straw mats lie just beyond the sliding shoji screens.

The older woman is standing just inside the house. She bows ceremoniously.

Turn to page 18.

The plane lands sometime in the afternoon at Narita Airport just ouside Tokyo in Japan. Surprisingly, the reception area is filled with fast-food restaurants and souvenir stores. The Japanese kids your own age, you are curious to see, are all wearing stone-washed jeans and sneakers; the adults are wearing Western clothes. You're not sure what you expected to see; something more exotic maybe.

Up ahead, a small figure is pushing his way through the crowd and waving.

It's Mr. Tanaka; he must have taken an earlier plane. He manages to get your group through customs, then to an outside, sunlit parking area where taxicabs, limousines, and minibuses are lined up along the curb.

"You take limousine to hotel," Mr. Tanaka says to Mr. Clark as he directs a uniformed attendant pushing a large airport cart loaded with your baggage. Then he bows. "Group all taken care of," he says.

You and the others get in the elongated limo. As it pulls out of the airport, it is immediately caught in congested traffic on the outskirts of the city. Up ahead, the tall, dazzling, ultramodern skyscrapers of Tokyo loom like the Emerald City of Oz.

Go on to the next page.

"That could be New York," Billy says. "If you look quickly."

"Whatever happened to the quaint Japan we used to read about in geography class?" Veronica asks.

"Maybe it's around here somewhere," you say. "It's not up ahead, that's for sure."

Turn to page 12.

Your kidnappers untie your feet and remove your shoes. Then you are taken, still blindfolded, into a building of some kind. You are led down several stairways and through many long corridors. Then your captors untie your hands, shove you through a door, and slam it shut behind you.

You pull off the blindfold. You are in a small, bare, windowless cell with a high ceiling. There are straw mats on the floor, and the ceiling is covered with a paper screen lit from above. A narrow panel at the base of the door slides open, and a red lacquer tray appears with an elegant cup, a teapot, and a bowl of rice and vegetables. A pair of chopsticks is included, and a napkin is artfully folded in the corner of the tray. If this is some kind of prison, you think, at least they feed you in style.

"What is your name?" a heavily accented voice asks from somewhere above the thin ceiling. "And where are you from?"

Turn to page 15.

"I still don't understand what this guy Kokuru is up to," you say. "We were sort of interrupted back in the castle while you were filling me in."

"I'll try to explain it this way," Aikiko says. "In some countries, even in yours I've been told, advertisers sometimes slip in a single frame of film advertising their products, either in films or on television. The frame goes by so fast that you don't see it with your conscious mind, but it registers on your subconscious."

"I've read about that. That's why people sometimes feel compelled to run out and buy a product that they don't really need or sometimes don't even want," you say.

"Exactly. It's illegal, and given someone like Kokuru, it can also be deadly."

"I wonder why the UJEC, Kokuru I mean, is sponsoring the karate tournament I'm supposed to be in," you say.

"That's one of his schemes I haven't heard about," Aikiko says. "But knowing Kokuru, whatever the reason, he's up to no good."

You come upon a group of small, one-story houses. They look contemporary, but they're also designed to harmonize with the more traditional architecture. Most of them are dark inside, with only faint glimmers of light coming from within. Only one, the largest of the group, is brightly lit. It's surrounded by a tall, weathered fence with a traditional Japanese-style gate. You approach cautiously.

Turn to page 83.

You go with the rest of your team to a nearby gym and practice. Over the next few days, Veronica and the others improve with each session. Even Billy is getting his old form back. You never felt in better shape, and Mr. Clark is becoming more and more optimistic about the chances of your team winning the karate tournament.

A few days later, and it's time. A UJEC van takes you to a giant circular sports hall. Teams are there from not only Japan and the United States, but all over the world. Everyone is paired off with an opponent. Veronica wins one match after another, as does Billy.

You are in top form. Your consciousness settles into complete tranquility, and you have no trouble dodging the attacks of your opponents. In fact, your mind is so calm that your attackers seem to be moving in slow motion. You easily move around them and strike the winning blows.

The rest of your team does very well, losing only one or two matches. As the tournament builds to its climax, your team ties for the lead. Eventually only one fight is left—a match between you and the Japanese champion.

Turn to page 9.

"We're in luck," Aikiko says, gesturing toward the cellular car phone. She dials a number, says something in Japanese to the police operator, and hangs up. "Help is on the way," she says. "I just hope they get here in time. We still may run into Kokuru's men."

"Look!"

About a quarter of a mile ahead of you, two cars are parked, one on each side of the road. Several men with guns are standing in the middle of the road between them.

"Kokuru's men," Aikiko says, speeding up. "I can recognize them from here."

The men look startled when they see one of their own cars bearing down on them. They jump out of the way as you roar past. You have a head start, but seconds later both cars are after you. A man with a gun leans out the window of the first car and starts firing. The back window of your car is suddenly starred, but it doesn't shatter.

"This car is probably bulletproof. Here, try shooting back with this," Aikiko says, handing you a gun she finds stashed under the front seat. "Aim for their tires."

Turn to page 60.

"The phone is dead," Aikiko says, coming back to the tokonoma.

"That's strange," the baroness replies. "It has always worked before. I can't imagine what could be wrong with it. After tea, I'll have Yumiko take you to another house and you can use the phone there."

"I hate to ask this after all your kindness," Aikiko says. "But could I talk privately with my friend for a moment?"

"Why certainly," the baroness says. "I will see how Yumiko is coming along with the tea."

Go on to the next page.

Aikiko pulls you into the office and slides the shoji shut. "The trouble with traditional Japanese houses," she whispers close to your ear, "is that they're all made with paper walls."

"What's going on?" you whisper back.

"I'm not sure. The phone not working could just be a coincidence. Then again, it may not be. Perhaps we should tell the baroness everything about our predicament. Our other option is to leave right away and keep moving. What do you think?"

If you decide to tell the baroness everthing,
turn to page 82.

If you decide to leave right away,
turn to page 105.

"I think we should get rid of the truck," you say.

Aikiko nods. "When I stop, we'll jump out and push it over the edge."

"We'd better do it now," you say. "The headlights are coming pretty close in both directions."

Aikiko turns the lights off. You can see the road ahead in the moonlight. The curve coming up provides the perfect opportunity to make your move.

Aikiko hits the brakes. The truck skids to a stop, the front bumper hanging on the edge over the steep drop-off. The two of you jump out and run to the back of the truck, giving it a push. Not much is needed. It falls over the edge, disappearing in the darkness below.

You start carefully down the rocks on the other side of the road, heading for the thick brush not far below. You're just in time; the other cars are almost on top of you. As you reach a ledge, you hear the screech of brakes from up above as both cars round the curve. A few seconds later you hear the sound of gunfire.

Turn to page 8.

"I told them that you were a new recruit and that I was assigned to show you around," Aikiko leans over to tell you as the two men confer. "Outsiders, they pointed out, aren't allowed in the labs. We're in trouble."

"What'll we do?" you ask.

"They're going to take us to the sergeant at arms on the upper level. Pretend to go along with them and wait for my signal."

Aikiko protests in Japanese as the two of you are led to the elevator. When the door opens, the men push you inside. As the door closes, Aikiko makes her move. Her hand is a blur as she knuckle-punches one of the men in the solar plexus—the area just below the chest. His eyes glaze over as he loses consciousness. The other man makes a lunge for the emergency button. Following Aikiko's lead, you push his hand away, at the same time using a backhanded strike to the side of his head, knocking him out.

"Well done," Aikiko says as she pushes the stop button. "I'll go down to the garage and see if I can grab one of their vehicles. I don't have much of a chance of getting away, but if I do, I'll send the police to come get you. Your best bet, I think, is to stay in the castle and plead ignorance."

You have a moment to think as she pushes the button for the lower levels.

If you insist on going with Aikiko, turn to page 30.

If you stay in the castle, turn to page 97.

The three of you go down to the lobby. Several cars are parked out in front. Mr. Clark and other members of the team get in the first one. The second one is also quickly filled. The remaining members, including Billy and Veronica, get in the third. You are about to slide in next to them when one of the drivers steps between you and the door. "Have special limousine," he says. "Take you to your meeting."

"Yeah, well our friend is with us," Billy says, trying to get out of the car. The driver gently pushes him back and closes the door.

Billy and Veronica peer out the window looking worried. "It's all right," you tell them. "I've been expecting this."

"If you would be so kind," the driver says, bowing. He points to a limousine parked off to the side.

You go over and get in as the driver holds the door open for you. A lone Japanese gentleman is in the backseat, beaming like a used-car salesman about to hook a customer. "So nice for you to join me," he says. "My name is Yoshi. I have an offer for you."

Turn to page 27.

The walls inside are made of stone, and one of them, you discover, is covered with weapons of all types—pistols, swords, knives, even machine guns.

"Looks like the baron was ready for anything," you say.

"That was a long time ago, and—" Aikiko starts, but she is suddenly silent as you hear the sound of heavy footsteps overhead. They are definitely not those of the baroness or Yumiko. It must be Kokuru's men, you realize.

After a while, it's quiet again. "Do you think they've gone?" you whisper.

"My guess is that they're searching all the houses in the neighborhood. They probably left someone behind to watch this one. Which gives me an idea. We'll wait a few hours, then surprise them."

There are several sleeping mats in the room. You doze until Aikiko shakes you awake. "It's time," she says.

Turn to page 55.

You relax your body and let the crowd take you wherever the flow goes. The pressure, though, increases from all sides, and soon you can hardly breathe. You've lost sight of Billy and Veronica. You can only hope they are all right.

Somehow, your legs get knocked out from under you. At first it doesn't make much of a difference since the crowd is holding you up, but then you start to sink, dragged down by the backward movement of the crowd. It's like being in quicksand. Your chin gets caught for a moment on somebody's belt as you continue to sink lower and lower. The last thing you remember before you lose consciousness is the top of a boot sliding past your nose.

Turn to page 87.

"What was that all about?" you ask. "Why'd you let me crawl out there and risk my life?"

"I was betting on the idea that if you tried to escape, you were not one of Kokuru's security people," Aikiko says. "Further, I suspect that you are one of Inspector Saito's agents, am I correct? You have a message for me from headquarters?"

"Message? Headquarters? I'm not security. I was kidnapped off the street just after I arrived from the States."

Aikiko is silent. "I see," she then says, as one of the elevators arrives. The two of you get in. "We have a problem. Why would Kokuru want you kidnapped?"

"I don't know," you say. "When I was in the electronics store in the city and those men in the strange-looking samurai costumes came in smashing everything up, I *did* see the face of one of the men when his helmet fell off."

"That must be it then," Aikiko says. "I've got to get back to the Tokyo police and tell them."

"Tell them what?" you ask.

"Tell them that the UJEC have started their plan to dominate the electronics market by wiping out the competition."

Go on to the next page.

"But how could they think they'd get away with that? Wouldn't it be kind of obvious?" you ask. "I mean if they destroy all the other name brands, won't people notice?"

"Oh, they'll smash up a few of their own things as well, just not as many. And that's only part of their master plan."

"Which is?"

"To conquer the world. I'll explain more later," she says as the elevator door opens. "First I want to show you something."

Turn to page 26.

After the meditation, the man leads a brilliant class, demonstrating many movements and techniques that you've never seen. Sometime during the class, you suddenly realize that you no longer care about what else is going on in the castle, as long as you can keep training here. You've finally found the true path to becoming a Master of Karate.

The End

武道

You, Billy, and Veronica run down the stairs to the basement. The salesclerk follows, pausing to slam the door shut behind him. You feel a sense of relief as he secures it with a heavy bar.

A single light bulb hangs from the ceiling of the large basement room, illuminating stacks of boxes. You can see from their labels that they contain electronic equipment.

Suddenly you hear a loud noise at the top of the stairs. The sound reverberates through the basement. "They must be trying to break down the door," Veronica says. "What do we do if they get through?"

Before you can answer, the store clerk frantically pushes boxes away from one corner of the room. He seems to know what he is doing. Behind the boxes is a tall but narrow opening. He motions for you and your friends to follow him inside. Above, you hear the door to the basement start to splinter.

"I don't know where this leads to," you say to Billy and Veronica, "but it beats staying here. Let's try it."

Turn to page 108.

Carefully you push open the trapdoor and climb out. Through an open doorway to the outside, you can see the early morning sun hanging just above the horizon. "Look at that," you whisper.

"That's why we call our country the land of the rising sun."

Slowly the two of you tiptoe to the edge of the shoji screen that separates the office from the main room of the house. There is no sign of the baroness or her servant. You hope they are sleeping peacefully in another part of the house.

"Be careful," Aikiko whispers. "These paper walls won't stop bullets."

Turn to page 25.

The noise of the traffic outside starts to get louder. You either must be in a city or close to one.

The car goes around a corner and pulls over to the side of the road. You feel the man on your right shift his weight and see him take hold of the inside doorknob. Your guess is that he's going to get out. This may be your chance to fight back. You're not sure what you are going to do, but you have only seconds to decide *if* you're going to do something. Despite your karate skills, you are still at a big disadvantage. The men holding you are big and possibly armed, and your hands are tied. However, doing *anything* might be better than giving up without a struggle.

If you decide to use your karate skills to try and escape, turn to page 84.

If you decide to wait for a better opportunity, turn to page 102.

Early the next morning, through a porthole just over your head, you see the sun rising. You manage to sit up enough to look out and find yourself on a calm sea somewhere. A number of small islands can be seen in the distance. As hungry as you are, you are more thirsty. Finally one of the fishermen comes below and gives you a cup of something. It quenches your thirst, but a few minutes later you begin to feel dizzy. Your drink must have been drugged.

Soon you start forgetting where you are and why you are here. The only thing you do know is that you are on a boat heading for some strange country—but you can't even remember where you are from.

Turn to page 10.

UNIVERSAL JAPANESE ELECTRONICS CORP.

Following the girl through the door, you find hundreds of students dressed in gis kneeling in rows, filling the large hall. Up front, a large movie screen covers the wall. The girl motions for you to take your place at the end of the back row.

As you do this, the screen lights up, and a man's face appears, filling the entire space. Speaking in Japanese, he begins a speech in the same booming voice that spoke to you earlier in the cell. Though the language is no longer English, you're pretty sure that it's the same man. The voice continues as the face vanishes, and you see an array of electronics products flashed on the screen, like a music video. Interspersed are shots of the Earth from space.

"UJEC, Universal Japanese Electronics Corporation. Today Japan, tomorrow the world," the girl translates for you.

Suddenly you remember where you saw that insignia on her jacket before—it's the logo of the UJEC! The voice in the room before was right, this is a coincidence.

Turn to page 23.

You've never handled a gun before, and you are surprised by the weight and size. You wish you didn't have to use it, but right now you have no choice. You roll down the window and point it behind you. When you pull the trigger, the gun almost jumps out of your hand. You manage to get off a lucky shot, and the front car swerves off the road and rolls over into a ditch.

The second car is still after you. You try for another lucky shot, but you miss, and this time the recoil from the gun knocks it out of your hand. Now what, you wonder, only to find out soon enough. A roadblock lies ahead. This time the cars are parked across the road.

Aikiko, however, lets out a whoop. "We're all right! Those are police cars."

When you reach the roadblock, Aikiko pulls over to the side. The car that is still chasing you slams on its brakes and makes a U-turn, speeding off in the other direction with two police cars hot on its tail.

A few days later, you get a letter of appreciation from the Tokyo police for helping Aikiko escape and foiling Kokuru and his scheme. It looks great framed on your bedroom wall next to your martial arts trophies. You now look forward to taking some time off from practice and being just a student, hitting only your books.

The End

"Friends all right," a man with a crew cut says in English. "They not badly hurt. You all very lucky."

"Who are you?" you ask.

"Businessmen," he replies. "Some call us *Yakuza.*"

"Yakuza!" you say. "I've heard of you. You're gangsters."

"No, businessmen. Maybe special kind of business, but—"

"I've got to find my friends," you say, swinging your feet off of the sofa and trying to stand up.

"Friends all right, I tell you!" the man says. "You must wait. Mr. Big on his way."

You feel dizzy and sit down again. "I think you've all been watching too many American movies," you say.

One of the other men says something in Japanese to the man with the crew cut. "Here comes Mr. Big now," he says to you.

At the far side of the office is an elevator. The indicator over the doors shows that it's on its way up. Suddenly the doors open, and the tallest Japanese man you've ever seen comes walking out. He is flanked by several smaller men—definitely thugs—who check the room out, then stand to the side, over by the windows, and look out as if they are expecting company.

Turn to page 76.

"All right," you say, grudgingly. "What is it that you want me to do?"

"Wait for the UJEC to contact you. Pretend to join their organization and keep your eyes open," Niko says. "We give you telephone number. You contact us later. Right now, go back to hotel. Not mention this meeting to anyone."

Two of Niko's men escort you toward the elevator.

"One more thing," Niko says. Rising from his chair, he grabs the left hand of one of his men and thrusts it in your face. Two fingers are missing, you notice. "Kano here fail on last assignment, pay Yakuza price. Now that you are 'associate member,' we hope you don't make any mistakes."

The elevator doors open, and you and the two men get in. One of them presses the button for the basement level, 34 floors down. When the doors open, a limousine is waiting for you.

Turn to page 101.

Before you can say another word in your defense, two of Niko's men drag you toward the desk and carry out the order.

"Now maybe you do better on your next assignment," Niko says over your screams. "We will contact you soon."

When you get outside, you take a cab directly to the hospital and get yourself bandaged up. You've missed the karate tournament and lost the end of your little finger. Enough is enough, you think. You waste no time getting the first plane back to the States. You can only hope Niko and the Yakuza have no way of ever contacting you again.

The End

You quickly stack the boxes on top of one another, carefully climb up, and look out the open window. You are aboveground, you realize, in some kind of castle. You see woods and farmland, and in the distance the lights of Tokyo in a bright, multicolored glow arching up in the night sky. Almost directly overhead a three-quarter moon emerges for a few seconds from behind the fast-moving clouds.

You lean out the window and look down. Projecting out a few inches from the wall is a ledge. Below that is a long drop to a moat or lake. It's dangerous, you think, but it's worth a try. You climb all the way out and find the ledge with your feet, flattening yourself against the building. Then you let go of the windowsill, working your way along the ledge, hoping to find a way to escape. It's tricky business. One slip and you'll plummet down 40 or 50 feet to the water.

In the shadows along the building you see a dark figure before you on the ledge. You are about to start back the other way when you hear a voice you recognize. It's the girl, Aikiko.

"You have done well," she says. "But now you must come back with me into the castle."

It's hard to tell what Aikiko wants of you. You can listen to her and find out. Or you can continue your escape by going in the other direction.

If you go back inside the castle, turn to page 21.

If you try to escape, turn to page 73.

You notice that Billy has his arm in a sling. He sees you looking. "It's not broken or anything. Just a sprain," he says.

You go inside, and Veronica runs over. "We were so worried about you," she says. "We got to the door of that game place and some motorcycle thugs attacked us. We didn't know what happened to you. The police came and cleared everybody out, but you were missing. What happened to you?"

"I'm not too sure myself. I got trampled and knocked out. I woke up in this gangster's office. He said that the UJEC people were—"

"The UJEC people, right," Billy interrupts. "They were here a couple of times this morning looking for you. I didn't tell them anything. I just said you weren't in."

"It must have something to do with the tournament," Veronica says. "You *are* the president of the karate club."

"Speaking of the tournament," you say to Billy, "how are you going to take part in it?"

"It's a couple of days from now," Billy says. "I'll be all right by then."

The phone rings, and Veronica picks it up. "Yes, we'll be right down," she says, and hangs up. "That was Mr. Clark. He says that the car is here."

Turn to page 46.

In the distance, rapidly growing smaller as you speed away, is the towering castle, pale in the moonlight, its curving roof outstretched like the wings of an enormous bird.

Suddenly you see a pair of headlights, like two glowing eyes in the darkness, coming in your direction—and fast!

"They're after us," you tell Aikiko. "Can we outrun them?"

"I'm not so worried about the ones behind us," she says. "What I'm afraid of is that they'll radio their agents and send a car to head us off." She pauses, then points ahead. "Look, down below—a pair of headlights coming our way."

"What do we do now?" you ask.

"We may have to abandon the truck and try to make our way down the rocks on the side of the road," she says. "On the other hand, that car ahead may not be one of theirs."

"How about stopping, turning off our lights, and then rolling the truck off the side of the road?"

"Good idea," Aikiko says. "But maybe we shouldn't abandon the truck. It's a long walk to Tokyo. What do you think?"

If you abandon the truck, turn to page 44.

*If you keep going in the truck,
turn to page 107.*

68

You dodge out of the way and strike back, cutting into your opponent's armor at the shoulder. A roar of approval goes up from the crowd. You guess that your opponent expected you to be an easy mark. He is much more cautious now, advancing on you slowly.

You avoid several of his attacks and manage to counter several times with your sword. Unfortunately your foot slips on the wooden stage, giving your opponent just enough advantage to finish you with a fatal blow. For what it's worth, you did put up an amazing fight against one of the leading swordsmen of Japan.

The End

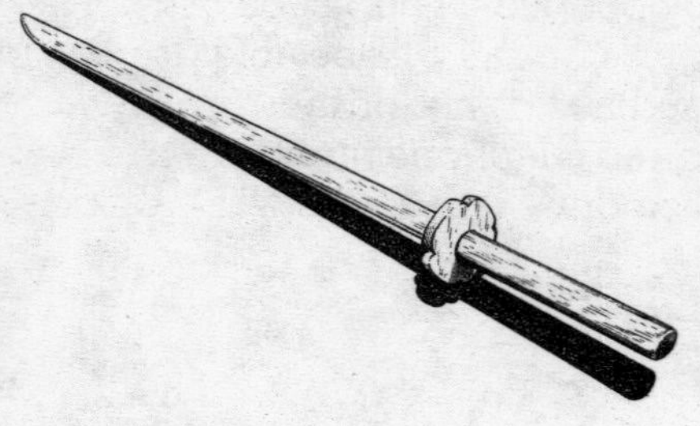

You and Tono walk up the wide, tree-lined main street of Kamakura. It leads to the major attraction of the city, the famous daibutsu—the great Buddha.

"Buddha statue once in a temple building," Tono says. "But building blew away in typhoon. People of Kamakura decided to leave Buddha out in the open for all to see."

"It sure is big," you say, looking up at it.

"The statue is thirty-six feet high and ninety-five feet wide. By the way," Tono asks, "how am I doing with my English? It is okay?"

"Your English is perfect," you say. "What I can't understand, however, is why those men were bringing me to Kamakura."

"Maybe they were taking you to a boat," Tono says. "But we'd better head back. You've got to catch that train for Tokyo."

Tono walks you back to the police station. There you say goodbye. "I hope you can get to America someday," you say. "I'll be able to repay the kindness you have done for me." You give him your address and telephone number in the States, then the police drive you to the train station.

Turn to page 86.

"I'll inform Mr. Clark of your whereabouts," Mr. Yoshi continues. "We shall be there soon."

"You mean we're going to the castle right now?" you say.

"No time like the present," Mr. Yoshi says. He says something in Japanese to the driver, and the limousine turns down a side street, which turns out to be just as crowded as the main one. What you've seen of Tokyo reminds you of a giant beehive. In the spaces between the massive skyscrapers, buildings are either being torn down or built. The whole city is in a constant state of activity and change.

After threading through numerous side streets, the limousine soon enters a district of low, one-story houses made of wood with contemporary tile roofs built in the Japanese style.

"I know you've had much training in kung fu and tae kwon do," Mr. Yoshi says. "We complete your training so that you also become master, true Master of Karate."

Turn to page 28.

You, Billy, and Veronica rush out through the back door and into the alley behind the store. At the far end, you see traffic and the flashing lights of the main street. You are about to head in that direction when a dark Toyota van pulls into the alley and stops in front of you. Several armored samurai figures jump out and dash toward you.

"Quick! Let's get back inside and down to the basement!" you shout. But as you try to get back in, several of the samurai come dashing out from inside the store. You run smack into one of them, and the two of you go tumbling backward, knocking off his strange-looking helmet. For a moment you see his head. He turns his head away from you and covers his face as he shouts something to the others in Japanese. Quickly they run over, grab you, and drag you into the van.

Turn to page 14.

You don't trust Aikiko, and you have no intention of going back inside. You back up along the ledge, hoping you'll be able to escape.

"I'm trying to help you," she whispers, approaching slowly.

"Sure," you say, moving away from her. As you back up, the ledge gets narrower. You barely have room to stand.

Suddenly you lose your footing and slip off of the ledge. Desperately you cling to the wall, but you can't hold on any longer. You plummet downward, hitting the water below with a splash.

You come up, gasping for breath, and start swimming for the castle wall on the other side of the moat. You are almost there when something wraps around your ankle and pulls you under.

You struggle to get free as another tentacle grabs you around the throat. What kind of creature has you in such a hold, you wonder as you are pulled deeper and deeper underwater. Unfortunately, you don't live long enough to ever find out.

The End

"Maybe the police would let me use the telephone," you say.

"I am sure they will," the young man says, then introduces himself. "My name is Tono."

On the way to the station, you tell him your name and why you've come to Japan. The rest of the story about your kidnapping he will hear soon enough.

When you get there, you tell them everything, with Tono translating. You ask them about Kokuru, whose name you heard mentioned often.

"They say that he is very important public figure. There is no way he could be involved in your kidnapping," Tono says.

Still, you have your doubts.

The police are very polite and let you use their telephone. You call Mr. Clark at the hotel and tell him a little bit about what happened. "I'll have to tell you the rest when I get back," you say. "The Kamakura police are helping me to get on a train back to Tokyo, so I should be there soon."

When you hang up, Tono says, "You will have an hour before you get the train. You must let me show you something of our city."

Turn to page 69.

Mr. Yoshi starts you on a tour of the castle. Each level has a different function, he explains. On some floors are very up-to-date laboratories developing chips for supercomputers. Other floors contain gyms used for karate and other forms of martial arts practice, including ninjitsu. After the tour, Mr. Yoshi takes you back to your room where a morning meal is waiting for you.

"I am pleased that you are with us," Mr. Yoshi says, bowing to you as he leaves. You bow back, suddenly feeling very important.

For the next few weeks you study advanced karate techniques, and even some ninjitsu, though you don't particularly like the philosophy behind the latter. You miss Billy and Veronica and wish you knew what they were up to and how they were doing. All the time, however, you store as much information in your mind as you can about Kokuru and his operations, knowing you'll eventually have to report back to Niko, the Yakuza boss.

Finally, sitting in your suite of rooms late one night, you realize that you must make a decision about your situation—do you have enough information to satisfy the Yakuza, or should you stay on longer and try to find out even more?

If you try to escape now, turn to page 98.

If you decide to wait and collect more information, turn to page 81.

The man called Mr. Big strides over to the couch, takes off his jacket, and hands it to one of the other men. Underneath, the sleeves of his shirt are cut off at the shoulder, leaving bare his muscular arms, which are covered with tattoos from the wrists to the shoulders.

"My name is Niko," he says, holding out his hand. "We shake like in your country. Make deal." Despite his Japanese accent, you have a suspicion that he is trying to do a Humphrey Bogart imitation, and a bad one at that. His handshake nearly crushes your hand.

"Glad you're okay," he continues. "Wouldn't want American tourist trampled to death. At least not in one of our respectable *pachinko* parlors."

"Pachinko? I've heard of that game. So that's what that place was," you say. "I'm all right now, so if you'll show me how to get out of here . . ."

"Not so fast. Have proposition for you," Niko says, snapping his fingers.

At once, two of his men push up a large video screen next to the couch. He snaps his fingers again, and Japanese followed by Western lettering appears. Surprisingly, it is information all about your life that appears on the screen!

"As you can see, we know all about you and your trips last year to China and Korea. In fact we are quite impressed by your talents," Niko says. "Apparently UJEC is also, otherwise they wouldn't have brought you here to be trained as their American agent."

Turn to page 24.

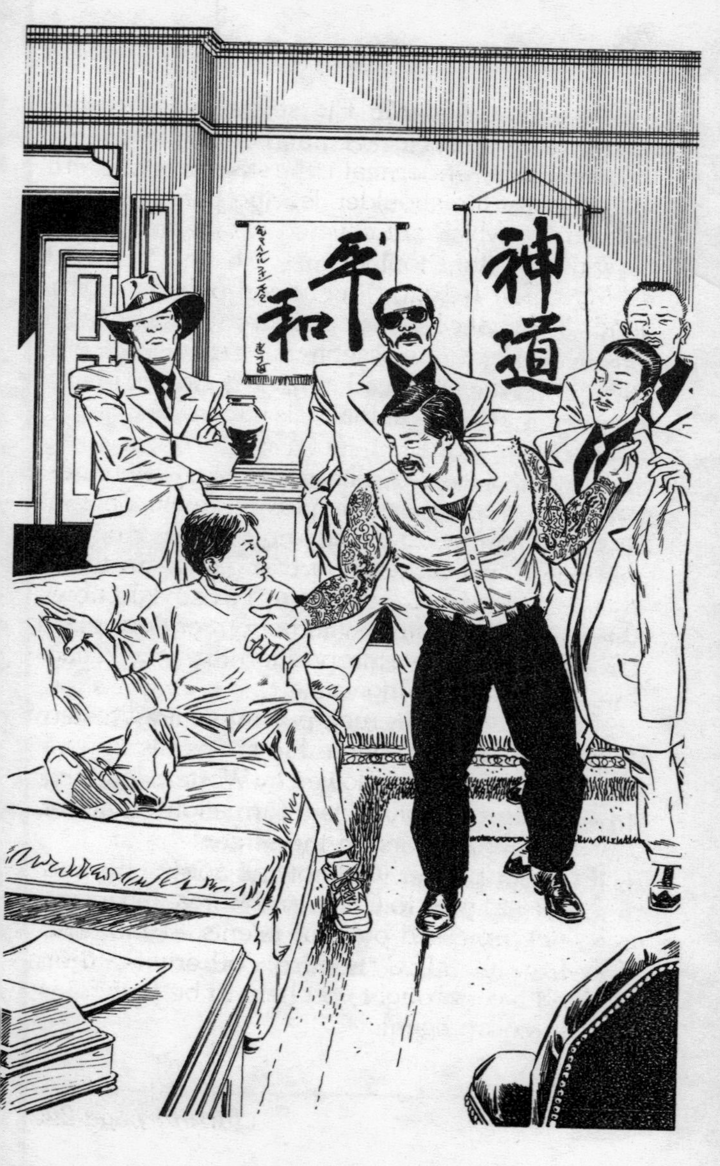
平和
神道

The next morning the ringing of a bell somewhere outside your room wakes you. Sunlight streams in from the garden where bright red flowers grow among the strangely shaped gray rocks.

You go into the bathroom, wash your face, and get dressed. As you are coming out, there is a knock at the door of your suite. It's Mr. Yoshi. "You are in luck," he says. "Mr. Kokuru, director of UJEC, will see you this morning, right away. He is waiting in office."

You hurry along behind Mr. Yoshi, down a long hallway, up a flight of stairs, and into a huge room. The walls are elaborately carved and gilded, and the dark hardwood floor is polished so that you can see your own reflection. You have no doubt that this was once the throne room of the castle. At the far end, however, instead of a throne, there is a large desk. Sitting behind it is a short, plump, Japanese man with a shiny bald head and a short, scraggly beard, dressed impeccably in a Western business suit.

As you walk across the room, he comes out from behind the desk with his hand outstretched. "Welcome to our organization and the world of UJEC," he says in perfect English, shaking your hand firmly and enthusiastically. "We Japanese are not known for getting right to the point, but I have learned this and many of your other Western ways."

Turn to page 22.

"I'm not joining anything unless I know what I'm getting myself into," you say.

"Very well," the voice says. "Then you will be dealt with."

There is silence for a long time. You sit there wondering what is going to happen to you. Eventually you fall asleep on the straw matting that covers the floor.

You wake up sometime later, when the door to your cell is opened and two men wearing black gis enter. Three more are standing outside. The odds are too much against you. You'll just have to wait for a better opportunity to make your move, you realize.

Without saying a word, they tie your hands in front of you again and blindfold you. You are taken out of the building and pushed into the back of a car. You are sandwiched in between the two men as the car takes off. They talk in Japanese, laughing frequently. You can't understand what they are saying, but somebody named Kokuru seems to be mentioned quite often.

The car keeps moving for what seems like an hour. The men are now silent, and your guess is that they're dozing. You take a chance and slip your tied hands up to your face, pushing the blindfold up slightly. They don't seem to notice. Looking down with your right eye, you can now see the legs of the man on that side of you and the lower part of the car door.

Turn to page 56.

You decide that the best thing for you to do is wait. There's more to be learned about the UJEC and its operations and about the martial arts before you report back to Niko and the Yakuza.

The next day, you start your training with the *bokken*—wooden swords. You put on the light body armor necessary for the practice. The swords look familiar; then you remember the men attacking the electronics store—they were using them!

You find that you have a lot of talent with the bokken. Even Mr. Kokuru comes to watch an exhibition match you have with Mr. Yoshi, who you discover is one of the top fencing champions of Japan.

Turn to page 109.

Deciding to tell the baroness everything, you and Aikiko go back into the main room just as she arrives carrying a teapot and several cups on a tray. Aikiko and the baroness both kneel on the *tatami* mat in front of the tokonoma, their knees tucked up under them. You follow their example.

The baroness pours some green tea into one of the cups and hands it to you. "This is not exactly a proper tea ceremony," she says. "Perhaps another time, if you visit again."

Aikiko clears her throat. "We have a confession to make. We did not have an automobile accident. We are trying to escape from some dangerous men. I am an undercover detective of the Tokyo police, and this is a friend who was kidnapped and taken to the castle."

"Ah yes, the castle. It has a bad reputation now, does it not? At one time it belonged to my family, dating back to the twelfth century. We are distantly related to the emperor, but through trickery and court intrigue, we were forced out by renegade samurai who then occupied it, terrorizing and exploiting the villagers of the area."

The maidservant, Yumiko, comes in and whispers something to the baroness.

Turn to page 31.

There are several breaks in the fence, just large enough for you to see through. You put your eye up to one and see a rock garden surrounding a small pool on one side of the enclosure. On the other side is a wide veranda. At the front of the house, *shoji* screens are pushed back, revealing an old woman in a brilliantly embroidered kimono, kneeling before a red lacquered table.

"What do we do?" you whisper to Aikiko.

"There are telephone wires leading to the house. We could ask to use the phone. On the other hand, there could be other people in the house besides the old woman. They may work for Kokuru for all we know."

"It is the closest house off the road."

"And it's all lit up," Aikiko says. "I wonder. It could be a trap."

If you decide to ask to use the phone, turn to page 32.

If you decide to keep going and look for a house farther away, turn to page 105.

As the car door starts to open, you spring sideways against the man on your left, using a body twist and your elbow to punch him in the stomach. At the same time, you give a snap kick to the back of the man getting out of the car. Your kick propels him out of the door and knocks him to the ground. You dive out of the car door and land on top of him. You manage to push your blindfold all the way off just as you hear the sound of a police whistle nearby. The man under you is still struggling to get up as a policeman and several pedestrians come running in your direction. With a terrific heave, he shoves you to the side and leaps back in the car as they arrive. The car roars away before he even closes the door.

The policeman helps you up and unties your hands with a look of amazement on his face. It must be unusual, you realize, to see a Westerner in Japan escaping from kidnappers.

"Are you all right?" a young man asks.

"I'm fine now," you say. "Where am I?"

"You are in Kamakura," he replies, helping you to your feet.

The policeman says something to the man in Japanese.

"He says he would like for you to come to the police station so that he can fill out a report," the young man says. "I will go with you and translate. I am a student of English and much appreciate the opportunity of speaking with you."

Turn to page 74.

Mr. Clark meets you at the station in Tokyo. "I don't understand," he says. "What were you doing in Kamakura?"

On the way back to the hotel, you explain in detail about the kidnapping and all that you have been through. Inspector Saito of the Tokyo police is questioning the other members of your team when you finally get to the hotel. You tell him about the raid on the electronics store and once again recap what happened to you.

"It's very strange," Inspector Saito says. "There have been a number of similar raids on stores, not only in Tokyo, but all over the country. One has even been reported in Hong Kong. You say that you saw the face of one of the men in the raid. Do you think you could identify him?"

"Definitely," you say. "Do you want me to look for him?"

"No, not right now. It is best for all of you to stay close together. It's safer that way. If you have any problems, call this number," he says, handing each of you a small card. "I'll be in touch."

Turn to page 39.

When you come to, you are lying on a leather-covered couch in a large office. Several Japanese men are looking down at you. They are dressed like gangsters in old late-night TV movies—dark suits with exaggeratedly wide shoulders, black shirts, white ties, and black-and-white pointed shoes.

"Where am I? What's going on?" you ask, trying to sit up. Your head feels awful. "Where are my friends?"

Turn to page 61.

"I accept your offer," you say, somewhat reluctantly.

The voice is silent.

"What happens now?" you ask, but there is no answer.

You sit on the floor and eat from the tray. You don't notice at first that the door to your cell has opened. When you look up, a small Japanese girl wearing a karate gi is standing there. A red insignia is stitched on her jacket. You know you've seen it somewhere before, but you can't quite place where. She bows ceremoniously as you get to your feet. Without speaking, she hands you a pair of cloth sandals and beckons for you to follow her.

As you enter the corridor, the floor, you notice, is made of a highly polished, deep red wood. The walls are of rough gray stone, and the ceiling is very high, covered with brilliantly lit paper screens like the one inside the cell you just came from. Suddenly a group of men and women jog past you from behind and head toward a large double door up ahead.

Turn to page 59.

You manage to get inside and close the door just as she floors the accelerator and takes off. Several men come rushing toward you from all directions, but it's too late. One of them bounces off the side of the truck just before it smashes through the wide wooden doors at the far end of the garage. Seconds later, the headlights are stabbing into the night.

The road curves ahead of you. The moon comes out from behind a cloud, and you see the roadway carved through a series of steep hills, spiraling down to the flat plain below.

"Looks like we made it," you say.

"So far. But Kokuru's men will be after us soon," Aikiko says. "Keep an eye out back and see if anyone is coming."

Turn to page 66.

"Look over there," Billy says after you've walked a few blocks. "It's an electronics store. Several electronics stores, in fact. They're all over the place!"

The three of you enter the nearest store.

"I've never seen so many different brands," Billy says as he heads up the center aisle of the showroom, which is curiously empty of people.

"Maybe we should just leave you here and come back in a few days," Veronica says sarcastically, but Billy is so engrossed that he doesn't even hear her.

You follow him to the back when suddenly there is a series of crashes in the front of the store. You turn around to see a number of figures dressed in some kind of black medieval armor. They are smashing the merchandise inside with heavy wooden clubs. The salesclerk hollers and runs through a door at the back of the showroom. You have no idea what's going on, but instinctively you, Billy, and Veronica follow him.

Turn to page 5.

A few days later, your team comes in fifteenth in the tournament, fighting top karate champions from around the world. "We might have won first place if you'd been able to compete," Mr. Clark says. "As it is, I think we did very well."

Veronica pats you on the shoulder. "As far as I'm concerned," she says, "you are still the Master of Karate."

The End

"What goes on here!" the referee shouts. Your opponent runs toward the exit. Several plain-clothes policemen rush to block his way. Before they can grab hold of him, the man scratches himself in the face with something in his hand and collapses to the ground.

Inspector Saito appears in the doorway and walks over to the man, bending down to feel his pulse. "He's dead," the inspector says. "Used strong poison in needle held under fingernail. Old Ninja trick. Now have difficult time finding who is behind all this."

"You mean he wanted to kill me?" you say.

"Apparently so," the inspector says. "It's a good thing you're well trained."

"You are also the new karate champion," Mr. Clark says, pumping your hand in congratulation.

The End

As soon as the referee steps back and the match begins, your opponent charges. You dodge his attack and try a flat-handed blow to the side of his neck. He blocks it with his arm and, at the same time, scratches something across the back of your hand. Your next movement, an instant later, is a closed fist punch that stops a fraction of an inch from his solar plexis, just below his chest. The referee jumps in, declaring this the winning blow. As he raises your arm in victory, you begin to feel weak.

Your opponent turns and walks toward the exit of the hall, but several plainclothes policemen move in on him before he can reach it. Inspector Saito comes running in from the outside. He walks over to the man, grabs him by the right wrist, and places him in police custody.

"Look under fingernail," the inspector says. "Small needle with powerful shellfish poison. You're lucky. One scratch and you would not have lived."

"But I did feel a—" you start to say, sinking to the floor.

Some luck. After all your training, your reign as champion lasts only minutes.

The End

Suddenly it hits you just how tired you are. All that you went through in that pachinko place combined with the jet lag is finally catching up with you. You take out the futon mattress and start to unroll it, when a girl wearing what looks like black pajamas rolls in a cart piled high with food, bows, and leaves. The timing is perfect—you're also starved. The tray contains, as far as you can make out, a bowl of rice with fried vegetables on top, some kind of soup, noodles, cooked fish, pickles, and several other dishes you don't recognize. You settle down to eat in front of the TV. Since there is no Western furniture in the room, you leave the futon rolled up and use it as a backrest. The food is delicious, even that which you can't identify. On the TV, many of the programs are reruns of American shows like *Magnum, P.I.*, and *Family Ties*, all dubbed in Japanese. It doesn't take you long to fall asleep.

Turn to page 78.

Agreeing to stay behind, you watch as the elevator door opens and Aikiko steps out. Nearby, a mechanic is working on a truck with the motor running. Aikiko dashes over, knocks the mechanic out of the way, and jumps in the driver's seat. Putting the truck in gear, she sends it hurtling toward the garage door. Two seconds later, Aikiko smashes through the door and disappears into the night.

A half dozen men rush toward the garage, shouting. A car heads out through the splintered door in pursuit of Aikiko. No one seems to notice you standing just outside the open doors of the elevator. You step back inside and push one of the buttons at random. The elevator doors close, and it starts to rise. The doors open into a large karate dojo. A Japanese man comes over and motions for you to take your place at the end of the row of students kneeling in meditation. It's like the beginning of your karate classes back home.

Turn to page 52.

You decide to escape. Forming a plan, you reach into the cabinet where your futon is stored and take out the black Ninja costume that they gave you, along with the Ninja hand claws. As you put them on over your clothes, you suddenly appreciate the UJEC for training you in ninjitsu.

Quietly you go out into the garden and climb up onto one of the tile-covered roofs. You move along easily, over to one of the outside walls, then work your way down like a shadow to the side of the drawbridge. Luckily a flatbed truck is just leaving the castle. As it goes past, you slip out of the shadows and jump on the back.

The truck continues on through the night. When it is at the edge of the city, you slip off and discard the Ninja costume. You find a subway station with a phone and call the number that Niko, "Mr. Big," gave you. He sends a car, and an hour later you are back in his office, high up in the downtown skyscraper. You tell him everything you've learned.

"You've done a good job," he says, flexing his tattoos. "Good, but not perfect. Maybe you should have stayed on longer. There are many things we still do not know about UJEC."

"I did the best I could," you say.

"I know," Niko says. "Because of that we only cut off small piece of little finger."

Turn to page 63.

ko to come back, you pull out ller boxes and make a comfortable urself, then lean your bag against the nderneath the high window. After a while, u doze off.

Suddenly the door bursts open. Several figures dressed in the same medieval armor as the ones who attacked the electronics store wore are standing there. This time, however, they're not carrying wooden clubs, but lethal-looking swords instead.

"Spy, we have come to arrest you," one of them says in English. "We know you are Aikiko's contact. We have already made an example of her. Now it is your turn."

They drag you to a room and roughly fit you into a suit of armor. You can barely see out of the helmet as they take you down a long hallway and shove you through a doorway at the far end. You find yourself on the stage of a large auditorium filled with spectators. A sword is thrust into your hand as another figure in armor charges at you from across the stage, ready to strike.

Turn to page 68.

You get into the limousine. It climbs up a ramp, out into the sunlight. Sometime later, you arrive at your hotel. The driver jumps out and opens the door for you. He is wearing a white glove, you notice, and you wonder if it is to hide missing fingers. As you get out, the driver bows. Before you can say another word, he is back in the limousine and driving away.

You enter the lobby and start across to the elevators when Mr. Clark comes running over to you. "There you are," he says. "We've been worried. Billy and Veronica said—"

"They're all right?" you ask.

"They're up in their room, resting. I heard how the three of you got caught in the middle of a gang fight last night."

"Gang fight? What gang fight?" you ask.

"Later. We are meeting with Mr. Tanaka in an hour. He is going to brief all of you on the rules of the meet," Mr. Clark says. He's sending a car to pick us up. Get yourself ready."

He goes off toward the street, and you go up in one of the elevators to the suite of rooms where your karate club is staying. Billy answers the door.

"You're all right!" he exclaims when he sees you.

Turn to page 65.

As the man on your right gets out of the car, you decide to wait and find out where you are first before you try to escape. A few minutes later he is back, and the car starts up again. It goes for another mile or so before it stops. You can see enough out of the bottom of your blindfold to tell that you are on a waterfront. You are parked next to a pier, and the two men holding you are joined by several others. Together they pull you out of the car and drag you over to what must be a fishing boat.

You are taken below deck, where they remove your blindfold, using it to tie up your feet. Dumping you into a hammock, they leave. You lie there the rest of the day and all of the next without food or water. You struggle with the ropes but can't get loose.

Turn to page 57.

The clerk disappears through the door as you, Billy, and Veronica cautiously climb up the stairs. At the top, you look out into a large, crowded room of people playing with what look like vertical pinball machines. They are filled with hundreds of tiny balls cascading down through a series of mazes.

The noise is deafening. The three of you try to squeeze your way through the crowd. As you get near the door, you become aware of some kind of commotion going on outside. You wonder if it has anything to do with the men who attacked the electronics shop. You hear a loud roar coming from outside—even louder than the noise inside! It takes you a few seconds to identify, then you recognize it as the sound of several motorcycles revving up their engines.

Whatever is going on, people from the outside are pushing to get in, even though the place is already jammed. You are pushed back. The crush is now incredible, although some of the people flattened against their machines are still playing!

You wonder if you should keep struggling to get to the door or if you should be passive, save your strength, and let the crowd push you back until you are in a position to do something.

If you fight your way to the door,
turn to page 110.

If you let the crowd push you backward,
turn to page 49.

You and Aikiko leave the house, sticking to the paths between the fields and avoiding any of the roads. Suddenly you hear what sounds like whispered voices ahead of you, though it's hard to tell amidst the chirping of the crickets. Aikiko senses danger and pulls you to the ground.

Suddenly a flashlight beam stabs out of the darkness, catching you and Aikiko in its light.

"Aikiko!" says a voice.

"We're all right!" she replies, getting to her feet. "This is my friend who helped me to escape. That's my boss, Inspector Saito," Aikiko tells you.

The inspector has a car with several of his men waiting on a nearby road. They give you a lift back to Tokyo.

"How did you find us?" Aikiko asks.

"Intuition and a little luck," the inspector says. "My men were dropping me off. I was on my way over to visit an old friend when we stumbled onto you."

Turn to page 113.

"I'm sorry, but I'm unable to join the Golden Ear Yakuza," you say.

"Yakuza respect your decision. Not respect those who join Yakuza out of fright, then try to leave or become stool pigeon."

"I guess I'll be going, then," you say.

Niko says goodbye, and one of the men escorts you to the elevator. You go down to the street level and try to find a cab outside.

I guess I misjudged those guys, you think.

Back at the hotel, you tell Mr. Clark about what you have been through. Billy and Veronica are all right, recovering from their experience in the pachinko parlor.

Turn to page 112.

You decide to stay with the truck and keep going. The cars coming after you are rapidly closing in from both sides.

Any doubts you have about the car in front of you go out the window when it suddenly swerves sideways, blocking your way. Aikiko slams on the brakes, but the truck doesn't stop in time, smashing into the car ahead. Her head hits the windshield, knocking her unconscious, while your door opens and you are thrown out onto the road.

Two seconds later, the car coming from behind rounds the corner at high speed. It too can't stop in time, and it smashes into the back of the truck, knocking it over the embankment, along with the other car in front.

Your leg feels like it's broken, but you get up painfully and manage to hobble back down the road. You don't get far. A hail of bullets cuts you down. There is no one left to explain the grisly scene when the police come.

The End

The three of you squeeze single file into a passageway, following the salesclerk. In addition to being narrow, it's filled with wire and pipes, some of which are very hot. Moving forward is difficult, and the passageway seems to go on forever.

Finally you reach what looks like another basement. Overhead, you hear the heavy beat of American rock and roll. The clerk goes up a stairway at the far end. As he opens the door at the top, the sound gets much louder.

Turn to page 103.

More months are spent learning the Japanese language. Eventually you acquire enough skill to speak easily with anyone in the castle. Meanwhile, you've become more and more convinced that Kokuru is your true master. After every one of his inspirational talks, you too jump to your feet and shout in unison with the others.

You look forward to the day when you can go back to the States and be an agent there for the UJEC—helping them with their plans to take over the world. You don't know that the Japanese police are about to storm the castle and arrest the top leaders of the UJEC—and you with them.

The End

You struggle through the crowd toward the front door. You don't know how you do it, but somehow you manage to make it. You find both Billy and Veronica; like you they've both seen better days.

In front of you, a dozen guys with shaved heads wearing black leather jackets drive their motorcycles around in a tight circle. You are trying to get out of their way when one of them drives his motorcycle over your foot.

Lying on the ground in pain, you hear police sirens coming in the distance. Suddenly the skinheads roar off, and all is quiet. Even the music from the place you just came out of is turned off. The chaos of only moments before seems as though it never happened. When the police arrive, you are taken to the hospital, where they put a cast on your foot. You'll be on crutches for several weeks.

Turn to page 92.

美容室
ハチンコ

A few days later is the karate tournament. You and your team win it easily. Afterward a representative from UJEC comes over to you with a job offer. "Nothing doing," you say. "The tournament was one thing, but Mr. Niko has told me all about your operations."

The UJEC representative turns pale. "Yakuza know about . . . UJEC operations?" he stammers.

"I'm afraid so," you say.

"Forget about UJEC offer. Must report to Kokuru right away," the man from UJEC says as he runs off.

"What was that all about?" Billy asks.

"I think I just avoided a lot of trouble," you say.

When you return home, you and your team are greeted as heroes. The school throws a big party for you where you are given the nickname Master of Karate.

The End

When you get back to the city, Aikiko's information and your testimony help put Kokuru behind bars and the UJEC under new management. Your reward is the top-of-the-line UJEC home computer. You decide to follow Billy's lead and become a computer buff for a while. It's much safer than karate, you figure.

The End

ABOUT THE AUTHOR

RICHARD BRIGHTFIELD is a graduate of Johns Hopkins University, where he studied biology, psychology, and archaeology. For many years he worked as a graphic designer at Columbia University. He has written many books in the Choose Your Own Adventure series, including *Planet of the Dragons, Hurricane!, Master of Kung Fu, Master of Tae Kwon Do,* and *Hijacked!* In addition, Mr. Brightfield has coauthored more than a dozen game books with his wife, Glory. The Brightfields and their daughter, Savitri, live in Gardiner, New York.

ABOUT THE ILLUSTRATOR

FRANK BOLLE studied at Pratt Institute. He has worked as an illustrator for many national magazines and now creates and draws cartoons for magazines as well. He has also worked in advertising and children's educational materials and has drawn and collaborated on several newspaper comic strips, including *Annie* and *Winnie Winkle.* Most recently he has illustrated *The Case of the Silk King, Longhorn Territory, Track of the Bear, Exiled to Earth, Master of Kung Fu, South Pole Sabotage, Return of the Ninja, You Are a Genius, Through the Black Hole, The Worst Day of Your Life, Master of Tae Kwon Do, The Cobra Connection,* and *Hijacked!* in the Choose Your Own Adventure series. A native of Brooklyn Heights, New York, Mr. Bolle now lives and works in Westport, Connecticut.